Dear Parent:
Your child's love of reading starts here!

Every child learns to read in a different way and at his or her own speed. Some go back and forth between reading levels and read favorite books again and again. Others read through each level in order. You can help your young reader improve and become more confident by encouraging his or her own interests and abilities. From books your child reads with you to the first books he or she reads alone, there are I Can Read Books for every stage of reading:

SHARED READING
Basic language, word repetition, and whimsical illustrations, ideal for sharing with your emergent reader

BEGINNING READING
Short sentences, familiar words, and simple concepts for children eager to read on their own

READING WITH HELP
Engaging stories, longer sentences, and language play for developing readers

READING ALONE
Complex plots, challenging vocabulary, and high-interest topics for the independent reader

ADVANCED READING
Short paragraphs, chapters, and exciting themes for the perfect bridge to chapter books

I Can Read Books have introduced children to the joy of reading since 1957. Featuring award-winning authors and illustrators and a fabulous cast of beloved characters, I Can Read Books set the standard for beginning readers.

A lifetime of discovery begins with the magical words "I Can Read!"

Visit www.icanread.com for information
on enriching your child's reading experience.

I Can Read Book® is a trademark of HarperCollins Publishers.

The Berenstain Bears at the Aquarium

www.icanread.com
Library of Congress catalog card number: 2011930718
ISBN 978-0-06-207525-3 (trade bdg.)—ISBN 978-0-06-207524-6 (pbk.)

13   14   15   16   SCP   10 9 8 7 6 5 4 3   ❖   First Edition

The Berenstain Bears®

at the
AQUARIUM

Jan & Mike Berenstain

HARPER
An Imprint of HarperCollinsPublishers

"Here we are at the aquarium,"
says Papa Bear.

"The what?" asks Sister.

"The ah-KWAIR-ee-um," says Mama.

"It is a zoo of the sea."

"There are many things to see,"
says Papa.

"I want to see the whale,"
says Brother.

"I want to see the dolphins,"
says Sister.

"What shall we see first?" asks Papa.

"The whale," says Brother.

"The dolphins," says Sister.

"First, let's see the fish," says Mama.

"This swordfish has a very long nose,"
says Papa.

"Pointy, too," says Brother.

"The flounder is very flat," says Mama.
"His eyes are on the same side,"
says Sister. "Ugh!"

"Here is a catfish," says Papa.

"It looks like a cat," says Brother.

"Here is a dogfish," says Mama.

"It does not look like a dog,"

says Sister.

"This way to the whale!" says Brother.

"This way to the dolphins!" says Sister.

In the next room they see an octopus.

"Which end is the front?" asks Mama.

"I'm not sure," says Papa.

They see jellyfish.

"Those long strings can sting you,"
says Papa.

"Not if we stay out of the tank,"
says Mama.

"Where is the whale?" asks Brother.

"And where are the dolphins?"
asks Sister.

"Look at those penguins swim!"
says Mama.

"Look at them dive!" says Papa.

"Why don't they fly?" asks Brother.

"Because they can't," says Papa.

"Why don't they walk?" asks Sister.

"Some of them do," says Brother.

"These are some big fish," says Papa.

"The sharks are very scary,"

says Brother.

"Look at their sharp teeth!"

"The sunfish is very funny," says Sister.
"Look at his big head!"

"The otters are so cute," says Mama.
"It is fun to watch them slide,"
says Papa.

"I wish I could see the whale,"
says Brother.

"I wish I could see the dolphins,"
says Sister.

The Bear family comes to the seal pool.

It is feeding time.

The seals make a lot of noise!

Their trainers give them fish to eat.

"This makes me so hungry," says Papa.

"Here is a place to eat," says Mama.
The Bears have lunch and watch
the seals.

After lunch, they spot a sign.

It says, WHALE AND DOLPHIN SHOW TODAY!

"Hooray! The whale, at last!"

says Brother.

"Hooray! The dolphins, at last!"

says Sister.

The show begins.

The dolphins jump and leap and spin.

The trainer tells them to do tricks.

The Bears clap and clap.

A whale leaps out of the water.

The trainer feeds him a fish.

The Bears clap and clap and clap.

What a show!

The trainer asks Brother and Sister
to help.

Sister tells a dolphin to leap.

Brother feeds a fish to the whale.

The whale and the dolphin
make a big splash.
The family gets all wet!

SPLASH!

"SPLASH!" yells Honey.

They laugh and laugh and laugh.